*T*his book belongs to

_____

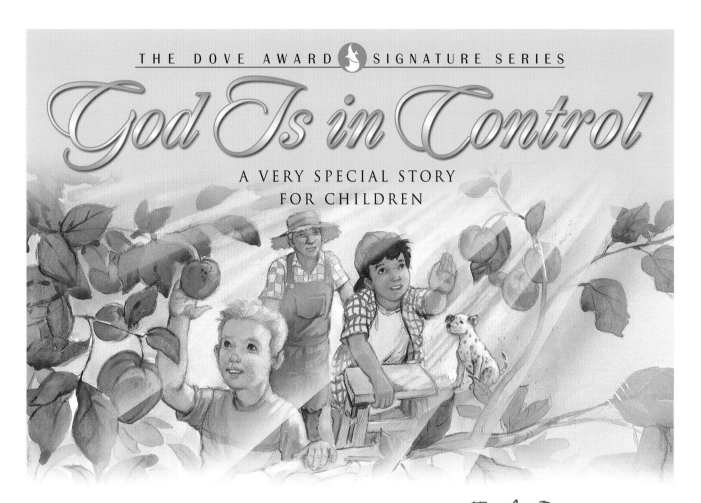

THE DOVE AWARD SIGNATURE SERIES

God Is in Control

A VERY SPECIAL STORY
FOR CHILDREN

BASED ON THE DOVE AWARD™ SONG BY *Twila Paris*

STORY WRITTEN BY STEPHEN ELKINS · NARRATED BY TWILA PARIS

ILLUSTRATED BY ELLIE COLTON

BROADMAN
&HOLMAN
PUBLISHERS

Nashville, Tennessee

With special thanks to Frank Breeden, Bonnie Pritchard, and the Gospel Music Association.

Song performed by The Wonder Kids Choir: Teri Deel, Emily Elkins, Laurie Evans, Tasha Goddard, Amy Lawrence, Lindsey McAdams, Lisa Harper, and Emily Walker. Solo performed by Lindsey McAdams.

Arranged and produced by Stephen Elkins.
CD recorded in a split-track format.

God Is In Control, written by Twila Paris © Ariose Music (ASCAP) Mountain Spring Music (ASCAP).
Administered by EMI Christian Music Publishing.

Copyright © 2001 by Stephen Elkins
Published in 2002 by Broadman & Holman Publishers, Nashville, Tennessee

Cover design and layout by Ed Maksimowicz.

Library of Congress Cataloging-in-Publication Data
Elkins, Stephen.
   God is in control / by Stephen Elkins ; illustrations by Ellie Colton.
     p. cm. -- (Dove Award signature series)
   ISBN 0-8054-2402-4
   [1. Stealing--Fiction. 2. Christian life--Fiction.] I. Colton, Ellie, ill. II. Title. III. Series.

PZ7.E4282 Go 2002
[E]--dc21
                                             2001043325

ISBN 0-8054-2402-4

1 2 3 4 5   06 05 04 03 02

This book is dedicated to the memory of those who lost their lives in the September 11, 2001 terrorist attacks. Though we see the devastation that comes from evil, we know that all things work together for good to those who love the Lord. God is <u>still</u> in control!

$\mathcal{T}$his is no time for fear. This is a time for faith and determination.

Paul knew stealing apples from Mr. Stephens' orchard was wrong, but all of his friends were doing it.

"This is going to be so much fun," boasted his friend Wally. "I've done it before and nothing ever happens."

"Why am I so afraid to speak up?" Paul thought.

7

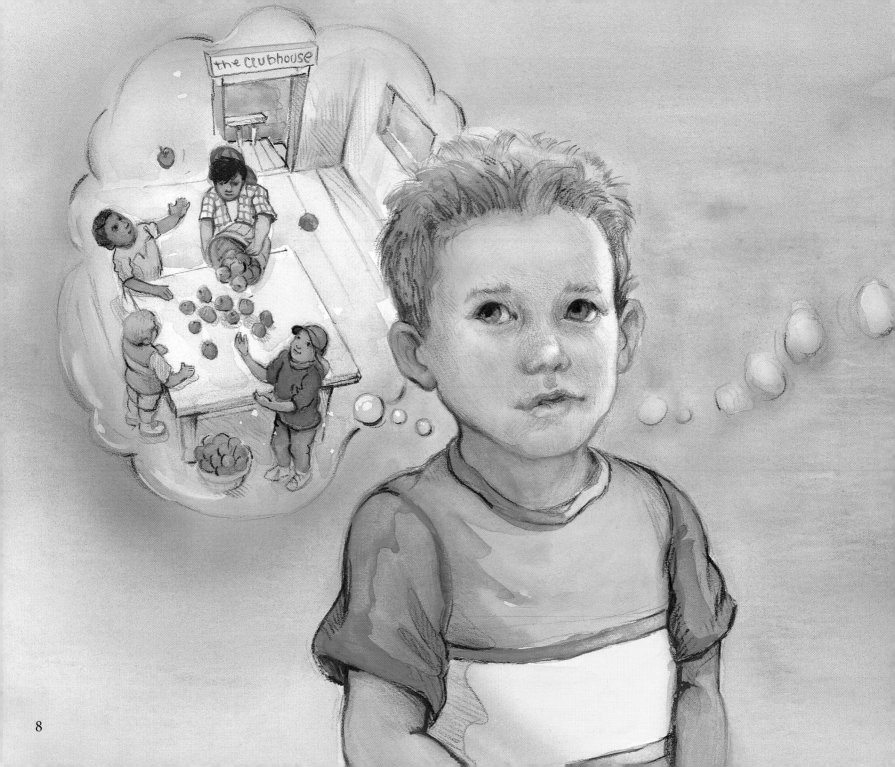

Don't lose the vision here, carried away by emotion.

"But what will my friends think of me if I don't go along with them?" Paul thought.

A decision had to be made. "Do I refuse to steal apples and risk getting laughed at, or do I go along with the crowd knowing it's wrong?"

9

Stephens'
Orchard

*Hold on
to all that you hide
in your heart.*

Paul knew what the Bible said about stealing and he was just about to speak up when Wally spoke again, "OK Paul, you and Mark go ahead and open the gate. Jenny and I will be right behind you with the baskets. It's apple pickin' time!"

There is one thing that has always been true. It holds the world together.

GOD IS IN CONTROL

And that truth is the Word of God. Paul knew this, but could he stand the test? His father had told him, "If you have to make a difficult decision, always ask God for help."

Paul whispered, "Lord, please take control of this situation."

13

*God is in control.
We believe that
His children will not
be forsaken.*

But before he could speak, Nipper, Mr. Stephens' dog came galloping out from the trees. Not far behind came Mr. Stephens' booming voice. "Nice of you kids to come by and check on my apples."

While the group stood frozen, Nipper jumped around, excited to see all the visitors.

Then Mr. Stephens said the most unusual thing.

*History marches on.
There is a bottom line
drawn across the ages.*

"And do you kids know what the bottom line is?" he asked. "The bottom line is character — having the courage to make the right choice, no matter what. You've all heard about Daniel in the Bible. He chose to be thrown in a lion's den rather than go along with the crowd!" Mr. Stephens continued.

Culture can make its plan, but the line never changes.

"God's Word is the line that never changes," Mr. Stephens said. "I suspect not all of you wanted to come to my orchard after school today, but you were afraid of what the others might think."

All of a sudden Paul blurted out, "I shouldn't have come Mr. Stephens. It sounded like so much fun at first, but it's wrong!"

19

No matter how the deception may fly.

"We have to hold on to our character," Mr. Stephens said as he put his hand on Paul's shoulder. "Some people might say it's not really stealing if you just take a few apples from the lowest branch. You may deceive yourselves, but you can never deceive God. Stealing is always wrong."

20

There is one thing that has always been true, and it will be true forever.

"A thousand years from now a person's character will still matter. Right?"

"Right!" they all shouted. "So kids, I assume you brought those baskets to help me pick apples for the church fellowship this weekend." They all looked surprised. "Just as I thought," Mr. Stephens continued. "We'd better get to picking before it gets dark." Then Paul had a thought about God.

*He has never
let you down. Why start
to worry now?*

GOD IS IN CONTROL

The Bible says not to worry about
tomorrow. Paul's Dad had even helped
him memorize that Scripture in the
book of Matthew. Now Paul under-
stood a little better what his Dad meant
when he talked about learning to rely
on God's strength in times of trouble.

Matthew 6

34 "Therefore do not
be anxious about ...

"Judge not ...

"Ask, and it will be given
... you. For every ...
to whatever you ...

He is still the Lord of all we see. And He is still the loving Father watching over you and me.

After a few minutes of picking apples, Wally spoke up, "Mr. Stephens, I need to tell you the real reason we came here today." "I know why you came," Mr. Stephens said. "But starting right now, we're all going to develop the kind of character Jesus wants us to have — bottom line character, right?" "Right," they all shouted. And Paul realized God had answered his prayer, because…

God is in control. We believe that His children will not be forsaken. God is in control.

As they picked apples, Paul kept thinking about how God really is in control of everything, and when we trust Him, God works out every situation for our good…and that truly is the bottom line.

God is in control.
We believe that
His children will
not be forsaken.
God is in control.

We will choose
to remember
and never be shaken.
There is no power
above or beside Him,
we know.

God is in control.

31

Don't miss the other titles in the Dove Award™ Signature Series for Children

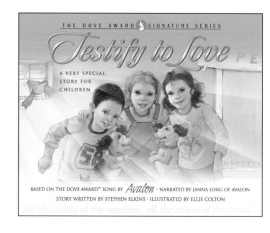

The Great Adventure
Based on the Dove Award™ Song
by Steven Curtis Chapman

0-8054-2399-0

Thank You
Based on the Dove Award™ Song
by Ray Boltz

0-8054-2400-8

Testify to Love
Based on the Dove Award™ Song
by Avalon

0-8054-2416-4

Available at Christian Bookstores everywhere.